THE TAIGA SYNDROME

Originally published in Spanish as *El mal de la taiga*
Copyright © Cristina Rivera Garza, 2012
Published by agreement with Tusquets Editores, Barcelona, Spain
Translation © Suzanne Jill Levine & Aviva Kana, 2018
First English-language edition, 2018
Fourth printing, 2023

Excerpts from this book appeared previously in *Fiction*, *PEN America*, and *Review: Literature and Arts of the Americas*.

ISBN: 978-0-9973666-7-9

Art on cover © Christine Ödlund, 2018
Dark Sun, 2011
Watercolor and pencil on paper, 72 x 53 cm
Courtesy Christine Ödlund and Galleri Riis

The publisher wishes to thank Robin Tripp

Design and composition by Danielle Dutton
Printed on permanent, durable, acid-free recycled paper in the United States of America

Dorothy, a publishing project books are distributed to the trade by
New York Review Books

Dorothy, a publishing project | St. Louis, MO
DOROTHYPROJECT.COM

THE TAIGA SYNDROME
CRISTINA RIVERA GARZA

TRANSLATED FROM THE SPANISH
BY SUZANNE JILL LEVINE AND AVIVA KANA

DOROTHY, A PUBLISHING PROJECT

I: The Same – 7

II: The Contract – 13

III: Going for Nothing – 18

IV: The Promise – 20

V: Everything Falls at the Same Rate – 24

VI: The Hidden Camera – 28

VII: Tongue to Tongue – 33

VIII: The Ferocious Wolf – 38

IX: There Is a Waterwheel Outside – 43

X: Dance Theory – 48

XI: The Pool – 53

XII: Those Things – 60

XIII: *L'Enfant sauvage* – 67

XIV: Placenta – 74

XV: Lap Dance – 79

XVI: Women Think Only about Sex – 89

XVII: An Underwhelming Face – 95

XVIII: I Would Be Stopped by the Dark – 101

XIX: Cruelty Never Is – 103

XX: Something Died Here – 108

XXI: The Large Window that Vibrates – 113

XXII: A Closed Forest – 117

XXIII: Playlist – 121

I: The Same

That they had lived there, they told me. In that house, there. And they pointed it out with an apprehension that could easily be mistaken for respect or fear. Their fingers barely peeked out from the cuffs of their heavy black coats. The smell of ash under their arms. Dirty nails. Dry lips. Their eyes, having discreetly moved toward where they were pointing, quickly returned to their original position, gazing straight ahead. "What are you really looking for?"—they asked without daring to say so. And I, who didn't exactly know, followed their steps like a shadow, back to the village over snow-covered trails.

It wasn't really a house, I should say first. I would have described what I saw on that morning, at the beginning of autumn, as a shack, maybe not even. A hovel. In any case, it was a habitable structure made from wood, cardboard, and lots of dry branches. It did have a roof, a ridged roof, and a pair of windows covered in thick transparent plastic instead of glass. It had the air of a last refuge. It gave the impression that beyond was only open space, and the law of the wilderness, and the sky, so blue, so high, above the wild.

I remember the cold. Above all, I remember the cold. I remember my clenched jaw, fists deep in my coat pockets.

They had arrived there, according to my information, at the beginning of winter. I had come to that conclusion because their last communication came from a telegram office in a border town about two hundred kilometers away. The telegram, addressed to the man who had hired me to investigate the case, said briefly and somewhat obliquely that they were never coming back: "WHAT ARE WE LETTING IN WHEN WE SAY GOODBYE?"

I took the case because I have always had an all-consuming weakness for forms of writing no longer in use: radiograms, stenography, telegrams. As soon as I placed my hands on the faded paper, I began to dream. The tips of my fingers skimmed the creases of the paper; the stale smell of age. Something hidden. Who would set out on such a journey? That couple, of course. Out of everyone, only those two. From what place, so far away in space, so far away in time, had this fistful of capital letters been sent? And what were the two of them hoping for? What had they let into their lives? That was what I wanted to know. From the start, that was what I wanted to understand.

The man had made an appointment with me in a café downtown, at four in the afternoon. I had only met him a few nights before, in front of images of a forest or of many forests. Oil paintings, X-rays. Installations.

"Do you like them?" he had asked me with an accent I wasn't immediately able to identify.

I told him the truth. I told him yes.

"Do forests intrigue you?" he asked me again, placing a hand on the wall I was leaning against. Where the back of my neck rested.

I turned to look at the painting to my right: oil on wood, wire, resin. A forest within a forest. Something primordial.

"They do intrigue me," I said, after considering it for a while.

"You don't seem like the kind of person who would get lost in a forest," he said as he took me by the elbow and, with a dexterity that was pure elegance, led me from inside the gallery toward the terrace.

"You're right," I told him. "Nor do I like being taken by the elbow," I added.

He laughed, of course. White teeth, Adam's apple quivering, the hint of a beard.

"Your face says that too," he said when he returned with two flute glasses.

I remember the toast, the first one. I remember laughing at a face I couldn't see—mine, which I was imagining so clearly. Its suspicious expression combined with a tacit sense of distance. My brow furrowed, my chin raised. I remember having said: "To the forest or forests." Glass clinking.

"But you must know about the Taiga Syndrome, right?" he asked after he had finally stopped laughing, after taking a large sip from the effervescent liquid in his glass. "It seems," he continued, almost whispering, "that certain inhabitants of the Taiga begin to suffer terrible anxiety attacks and make suicidal attempts to escape." He fell silent, though it seemed like he wanted to continue. "Impossible to do when you're surrounded by the same terrain for five thousand kilometers," he concluded with a sigh.

I remember the wolf. I saw him, an enormous wolf, gray against the snow. I saw his jaw: open. His eyes, his paws. I saw the red thread that extended from his tracks and slithered through the snow before momentarily getting lost in the trunk of a fir tree. I saw the fir, so majestic. Then it climbed, the red thread, through the warped branches, through the evergreen pine needles until high above it reached the green branches of another conifer. That was what made me look up at the sky, also gray, filled with thick jumbled clouds. What shade of gray? Ten minutes before a storm gray, of course. I didn't hear anything, couldn't hear anything, but I saw that the wolf was preparing to pounce. I saw his saliva, teeth, lips.

"The same," I repeated, attempting to rein in the threads of the conversation.

"The same," he said, recognizing my effort. "If you don't catch them, wrestle them down, like in rugby, they might vanish forever in the immensity of the Taiga."

"The same," I repeated. Sometimes seeing is just the confirmation of a fact.

It is difficult to know for sure when a case begins, at what moment one accepts an investigation. I suppose that, although the exchange of information and the negotiation of my contract didn't happen until days later, on a summer afternoon, in the downtown café of a coastal city, the case of the mad couple of the Taiga began right there, on the terrace of a gallery where a man with the hint of a thin blond beard had taken me by the elbow without my consent.

II: The Contract

He had heard of my work, that's what he said. He already knew about me when he took me by the elbow to cross the gallery and lead me toward the terrace. Had I noticed how dark the sky was that night? Had I known that the artist who painted/installed/sculpted/photocopied forests had told him I was, in fact, a detective?

As we talked, he drank his coffee and looked around. As we talked, he lowered his eyes and placed small cubes of sugar in the dark liquid. A spoon. Circles. Sometimes this is what being nervous looks like.

"It's been a while since I worked," I said. Though what I really wanted to say was: "Don't you know about my many failures?"

The case of the woman who disappeared behind a whirlwind.

The case of the castrated men.

The case of the woman who gave her hand, literally. Without realizing it.

The case of the man who lived inside a whale for years.

The case of the woman who lost a jade ring.

"It's better this way," he said, as if he had heard me say something. Then, without missing a beat, he placed a leather briefcase on the table and began to open the lock with his long nervous fingers.

It was then that I saw the telegram, their last written message. There it was, on top of a pile of neatly organized documents: letters, maps, tickets, transcriptions, photocopies, envelopes. Sometimes, everything exists for the first time.

"I haven't said yes," I said as I touched the papers. "It's been a while," I insisted.

I remember how warm the wind was. The way the white linen curtains announced the proximity of the sea. Above all, I remember the salt. Opening the windows wide. I remember that the salt told us who we were. Or how.

"I lost a woman," he murmured. "She left with another man," he added, his voice faraway as if he were struggling to remember language. "They both left, I mean." Forcing the words out was more physical than emotional, every word a strike ushered viciously from his mouth, every word a lethal blow. "I am terrified they might be like the mad people from the Taiga, the ones I mentioned before." His smile emphasizing that he meant to ridicule them, or worse, himself: "I told you about them, I'm sure you remember."

I remember, above all, the shame. The definition (from old English, *scamu*): 1. A painful feeling of humiliation or distress that typically inflames the face, caused by being conscious of behavior—either one's own or others'—that is wrong, ridiculous, or foolish. I remember what I saw in his eyes.

"Your wife?" I wanted to know as I touched the documents without daring to read them.

"My wife, exactly," he answered. "My second wife. The first one died in an accident, years ago," he said before I could ask.

I looked directly at him, intrigued. I swapped my

coffee for a glass of wine. I ordered rye bread, olive oil, balsamic vinegar. I asked for water.

"I am older than I look," he assured me.

"How old?"

"Older than you might imagine, Miss," he said.

It always surprised me that he was so formal, but the anachronism had its charm. In fact, it made me treat him more formally as well.

"Sometimes, Sir, you have to let wives go," I said. "Especially second wives."

"If that's what she really wanted," he interrupted, "would she be sending me messages from everywhere she goes?"

In the photograph he held in front of my eyes the woman seemed happy. Her smile, at least, was enormous. Contagious. Something viral. In fact, it was a series of images. The photographer had captured, second by second, the way the woman spun on her own axis. Her red dress, opened. Again, her smile. And in the background, the forest.

"So, is she Hansel or Gretel?" I asked, truly curious, still staring at the images.

"Gretel, I suppose," the man hesitated, taken aback.

"Maybe she is the woodsman or the witch or the woman who wants to get rid of the children in order to have enough to eat," I said more to myself than to the man who had begun to smile, stupefied.

"This is not a fairy tale, detective," he said, interrupting me again. "This is a story about being in love."

"Or being out of love," I corrected him.

III: Going for Nothing

I remember what I meant to tell him in that bustling café whose windows were grazed by the ocean salt, that clingy, inescapable substance that reminds us who we are—or how we are—when we feel it on our skin or tongue. Instead of taking the money from his hand and nodding in agreement, I remember I wanted to tell him that, in the end, no one knows why someone leaves. No one can be sure.

But I took the money and I took the briefcase filled with documents and I told him yes. I would take the case of the mad couple of the Taiga. I would solve his riddle. I would say to him, at the end, many days later, when my hair was much longer, that no one ever knows why. That on some days, being out of love looks the same as being in love. But I think I took his money and the briefcase full of documents and agreed because I wanted to come back and tell him that, in the same way, just like being in love, being out of love also ends one day.

You go for nothing if you really go that far, that's what someone said in an old song. I remember that I remembered—or might have remembered it.

IV: The Promise

That it had been a long time since I investigated anything was not a lie. Failures weigh people down. Writing reports of all the cases I was unable to solve, however, had helped me to tell stories, or at least get them down on paper, as they say. Whether I was obeying or taming language is not important. I hadn't taken an official job anywhere, but instead had begun to lead the discreet life of a writer of noir novellas. Sometimes failures push us to open the door of a run-down old house, to clean the dust off the unused furniture and find a drawer where an old typewriter hides. Failures force us to reflect, and reflection, with any luck, may lead us to a coastal city and a pile of blank pages. Failures drink coffee in the morning and keenly observe the afternoon light, and, when possible, go to sleep early.

I busied myself organizing a small house that I had abandoned years ago and dedicated my time to writing about the cases I had worked on, but I wrote them differently. It wasn't that I solved in my imagination what I was unable to solve in reality. It wasn't that my dismal figure transformed, thanks to the grace of fiction, into a glamorous heroine or an ill-bred villain. My new method was to recount a series of events without disregarding insanity or doubt. This form of writing wasn't about telling things how they were or how they could be, or could have been; it was about how they still vibrate, right now, in the imagination.

When I finished my first manuscript, I sent it out to a small but prestigious press that published novels of a similar style. I added a brief letter of presentation, and without imagining what would happen, I stuffed all the sheets of paper into an envelope and sent it off.

I recall that I was eating an apple while doing this. I remember the dreadful noise made by my teeth as they sank into the fruit and the even more dreadful noise when my jaw tore off the first bite. Above all, I remember the noise the package made as it slid down the mail slot.

. . .

That the painter of the forests had told anyone I was a detective seemed strange to me, to say the least. Everyone knew I had left that phase of my life behind. Though no one, that I was aware of, knew about the agreement I had made with the editor of the small press who had written to offer me a publishing contract. In fact, this editor had helped devise a plan to protect my identity: I would use a pseudonym and, in order to avoid the perverse curiosity that sometimes comes with anonymity, he would hire a woman approximately my age, with a somewhat similar appearance, who could answer questions in interviews and readings. Meanwhile, I could continue to live in the old house by the coast, telling stories to an ancient type-writer, thinking. The agreement seemed acceptable.

If I hadn't liked the man, if he hadn't taken me by the elbow in order to cross the gallery and arrive, somewhat out of breath, somewhat astonished, on the terrace, I certainly wouldn't have accepted a case that was so dull and hopeless—a case like so many others.

"Bring her back" is what he asked of me. Only that. "Go to the Taiga and find her and when you do, please, bring her back."

I promised him I would, without taking my eyes off his Adam's apple that rapidly rose and fell. I promised him I would, while my hand, of its own accord, reached out to caress the hint of a beard on his chin, then his left cheek. What's true is that it was a very dark night.

V: Everything Falls at the Same Rate

That I would study the documents very carefully, I told him many times. I would read everything, I said, and when I said this I must have lowered my eyes. Modesty is an unyielding stone somewhere deep in the chest. That I would open a new folder and aptly name it "The Taiga Syndrome" in order to record, in different fonts, doubts, discoveries, loose threads. Hunches. I would find her. Yes, I would find them.

I remember the sound of the blades as the helicopter circled the house while I flipped through the loose sheets of paper. I remember how I raised my face to try to look through the ceiling. And why doesn't he go himself? I remember asking. What is he afraid to face?

It took me three days to form a rough idea of what the Taiga actually was. Its temperature, its flora, its fauna, its shades of green. The names of its provinces and the names of its cities and towns and backwaters. Its language and languages. Its rivers. Sometimes it is good to remember that we all live, after all, on one planet.

The telegrams and letters helped me to reconstruct their route. Postal stamps. Their ink sometimes smeared by the rain and snow, at other times crisp and clear across space, across time. The man was right: The woman seemed determined to be found. Like Hansel or Gretel, or both, she had sprinkled crumbs of words in every telegraph and post office they passed through. As they progressed, the cities shrank and the transportation became increasingly rudimentary. Airplanes. Trains. Ferries. Barges. Rowboats. Kayaks. She gave the impression of being unable to stop. As if she were falling; it was the same with the messages, as if they were falling. In truth, what she seemed to want was for someone to catch her, to wrestle her down, like in rugby.

I remember the physics lesson that came to mind when I started to read the telegrams: How, not factoring in the presence of air, everything falls at the same rate.

How the force of gravity has been explained. How an object accelerates when near an astronomical object. Weight. Attraction. A certain speed. Everything falls at the same rate. I remember that I searched for a quote from Einstein where he likened gravity to fiction: "Said force is an illusion, an effect of the geometry of space-time. The Earth deforms space-time to its own environment, in such a way that space itself pushes us toward the ground."

No one can really know why a person leaves their home, not even, or especially, the one leaving. But why would anyone follow someone else to the Taiga? The answers, for me, were many. For money, of course. For an Adam's apple that threatened to break through the leathery skin of a man's throat? That as well. In order to have the opportunity to ask a woman, directly, while grabbing her by the right arm in a struggle that was nearly pointless and even less decent, why, what for? Yes, for that also. Also. In order to see her eyes, terrified. In order to sink into those eyes, an insect of the boreal forest. Something tiny that stings or bites. In order, once inside, to trigger that buzz. To lodge inside her the question or the complaint: Tell me why. Tell me where this passion comes from. How, why, of what is it made?

VI: The Hidden Camera

That they had arrived together and in a deplorable state, they told me from the beginning. It was obvious they had been crossing the Taiga on foot, probably for days, aimlessly, until they stumbled upon the village by pure chance. A couple of lunatics infected by the Taiga, demented or delirious, it doesn't really matter. In the report I would write for the man who had had two wives, I would assure him that the inhabitants of this village, which lay at the entrance of the forest right on the border between the Taiga and the tundra, had taken them in out of pity.

I would repeat the word: pity.

Spectres more than ghosts was how they were described. Skeletons more than actual bodies, they told us again and again. If their physical state had been different, the villagers would have thought they were criminals or fugitives. But when they first arrived, they were simply taken for a pair of lost children. Their hair, filthy. The searching look in their eyes. The high gaunt cheekbones. No doubt something or someone had eaten whatever crumbs they might have left behind them. The path of their return.

Scholars of Hansel and Gretel argue that the original story by the Brothers Grimm was a warning against the brutality of life in the Middle Ages, a time characterized by a hunger and scarcity that with frequency, with terrorizing frequency, led to infanticide. These scholars add that the story of Hansel and Gretel as we now know it is only a sterilized version created for the middle-class sensibilities of the nineteenth century. In fact, they insist that in the first versions written by the Brothers Grimm there was no stepmother at all; instead, it was the mother herself who persuaded the father to leave the children in the forest to starve to death. This change, the experts explain, this deliberate lessening of violence against children, seems to have occurred in order to prevent certain refined and modern mothers from being forced to hear the stories of other mothers, no doubt desperate mothers, perhaps savage mothers, unnatural mothers, one might say, who had mistreated their children to the point of death. On the other hand, everything seems to indicate, at least in the story of Hansel and Gretel, that the mother or stepmother and the witch, whom the children kill in the end, are the same woman transfigured. Proof of this shared identity: Besides placing the children in danger, the two women share the same preoccupation with food. In the case of the mother or stepmother, it manifests in her attempt to prevent hunger, while with the witch, whose house is made of food, it is seen in her desire to consume the children.

But these kids, these missing children of the Taiga, had chosen to flee—all by themselves. There was no desperate violent mother hovering over them. No hunger surrounding them. These children had left everything behind in order to burrow into the forest and escape themselves. From themselves or to themselves, it did not matter. Were they, then, their own mother and their own stepmother—or their own witch? All of them transfigured?

I remember the fear. It was the first time I had ever felt that type of fear. I turned my head to the right and then to the left. I looked at the ceiling of the cabin. Something was close by: I sensed it immediately. A threat. Maybe a hidden camera that watched me from above or from a distance. A hidden camera! I remember the laugh that followed that idea. The crazy laugh. No doubt the laugh of the Taiga. I remember that I asked them, as if it were relevant, if they had electricity. I remember their response: a lit candle. Was it fear or just a general state of alertness I felt? I remember asking myself that.

The truth is, reading someone else's journal teaches you very little. Before leaving, I had carefully read the woman's diary and yet had very little sense of who she was or what she was seeking. I had, I suppose, as little an understanding of her as she did herself while writing. Journals, I had to remember as I flipped through the pages, are written in an intimate code capable of escaping the reader's—and often the writer's—understanding. The woman. I did carry a few of her images in my head, for example the recurrent image of the forest, the word "coniferous," the word "boreal." The word "footpath." All together, they constituted something like a mantra, or the sentimental beads of a rosary. When nothing else seemed to make sense, sense was hidden in irrefutable words: a sliver or the space for a sliver. Beneath the overcast sky, another recurrent image. To live inside a cloud, she sometimes said. She was either praying or begging, it didn't matter. At what moment does a cloud turn into a million drops of mist? She was asking, not me. A face looked up, toward the sky, mouth opened. I carried another image of her with me: the image of a swimming pool, a diving board and ice. On top of the taut diving board, barefoot. Below, transparent water covered in golden leaves, the pool. Would she jump? I was asking, not her. The ice: all around but just beginning to take shape. Just a premonition: in any case, something invisible. Gray and white storm clouds through the branches of the trees: firs, birch, cedar.

VII. Tongue to Tongue

Among other things, I should explain that all of this occurred at the beginning of autumn. That the wind blowing my hair was icy, nearly freezing. That the pool caused curiosity, or terror. A pool in the middle of the forest, through the mist, how could this be? All these images and the long journey toward these images ended, essentially, during the last days of summer, already turning little by little at first, then all at once, into autumn. Before, I had bought the plane tickets, the train tickets, passage for the barge. Whenever it was possible from faraway, electronically, I had made reservations at hotels and hostels, for single rooms. I contacted friends who put me in contact with their friends who little by little brought me closer to the Taiga. It was necessary, as it is always necessary, to find a translator. A guide. So, long before I arrived, even long before I left, I had among my contacts a speaker of their tongue who would put everything into my tongue.

. . .

I remember how many times I repeated the same phrase:
a speaker of their tongue who would put everything into
my tongue. A smile, no, a laugh. Tongue to tongue. A
look of intrigue or distress; a sigh or something more
serene.

In the report I would write for the man who had had two
wives, I would ask him to take into account that nothing
had happened exactly as I claimed. I would tell him that
nothing happens as it is written, and I would constantly
repeat this or something like it. I would ask him, in a care-
ful and tactful way, assuming that he knew but realizing
also that these types of things are always hard to bear in
mind, to take into account that there was a great distance
between speech and writing. Take your time, I would
remind him. Read as if there were many minutes, even
hours, between the words spoken and the ones written
down. Transcribed. The phrases. I would tell him—for
example, when I wrote: "I asked them if they had electricity and they responded by showing me a lit candle"—that
he should realize I had, in fact, pronounced that question,

but before I received the answer, which came much later, the translator had made me repeat the question several times, and then had said it several times himself until the inhabitants of the village in the Taiga could understand it and answer. And then we had to wait—translator, villagers, myself—until the action, showing the candle and articulating the words "we don't have electricity," was heard and understood, first with surprise, and then, finally, disbelief.

I remember the image of the abyss. Above all, I remember the words "world's end" strung together. The images of my own city, a place of dark corners that I, like the couple, had left behind.

The translator waited for me at the airport of the last city the couple had visited before continuing into the little towns of the Taiga. From there, from that border city, the following telegram had been sent: "THE DISTANT NEVER SO CLOSE." I imagined they must have landed at that same airport, buttoning their coats and wrapping scarves around their necks, and they must have taken a moment to look at the sky. I'd never know if this was actually true. I'd never have any idea of how long it took them to find the man who drove them. To where? I imagined that they must have slept there, in that city of 200,000 people, where oil is extracted, but I wasn't sure about anything. The only certain thing, the only evidence, was that from this city a telegram full of capital letters was sent. A telegram but also a letter. A very brief letter written in pencil by a hand that seemed timid or weary, "NEVER DID THE DISTANT STRIKE SO CLOSE." The variations continued.

The translator did not smile when he saw me, but he did stretch out his arm to shake my right hand. He said something in my language but upon realizing that I had difficulty understanding, he chose to use the language that we would speak during our journey through the boreal forest: a language that was not strictly his nor mine, a third space, a second tongue in common. The translator was a relatively small man, thin and only a few centimeters taller than me, with an impenetrable expression. If I had not been aware of his hunting expertise and his various jobs on fishing boats and in the lumber industry, I might have thought he was a fragile man. When he shook my hand, I could feel the coarse skin of his palms and the rough tips of his fingers. Calluses. Our first exchange led me to think of him as taciturn. Like a tree that at first glance appears dry or dead. His salary, which had seemed meager to me, had freed him, momentarily, not just from a limited existence, but also from the sedentary nature of urban life to which he'd had trouble adapting.

"I come from over there," he told me, pointing out a vague area on the horizon that I had to imagine was the Taiga. Our destiny. He motioned for me to follow close behind him and began to walk, not looking back.

VIII: The Ferocious Wolf

That the first person we were able to get to talk to us was a young woman with short blond hair didn't surprise me, I would note in the report I would eventually write for the man from the coastal city. Sometimes the best informants are women and children. The unemployed. The absentminded. The villagers had decided to let us stay in the same cabin that had been occupied, months before, by the couple who had emerged from the forest one fine day. We never learned how the villagers made this decision. We didn't know if the decision came from a last-minute community meeting organized in haste when they learned of our mission, or if it had been made by some leader who had consulted with their powers-that-be, whatever this power consisted of for them, wherever it was or whoever held it. What was clear to the translator and to me was that by staying in the cabin, which the villagers had pointed at with respect or terror when we arrived, we were being reduced to the same condition as the pair we were looking for. Excluded. It became clear that for them we were *others*. Another pair of beasts or lunatics. People who could not be accounted for. When they opened the door to let us look inside the cabin before going in, it seemed as if there were some urgency. When they shut the door behind us and left in a hurry, it was clear they wanted to avoid contact with any person or thing having to do with what they called "the Taiga couple."

The woman knocked on the door a little after midnight. She apologized, lowering her head. She asked to come in and once inside took off her hat and asked to sit on one of the two chairs around the small wooden table, just a few centimeters from the bed where they, the others, had slept, and where we would be sleeping. A mattress on the floor. I sat on this bed, leaving the other two around the table.

"We never could explain the smell," translated the man while the young woman sat and began brazenly sniffing. "As if someone died here, right?" she said in a low whisper, allusively, leaning her face over the candle.

"Could someone have died here?" I asked, intrigued. "Did someone die here?" I insisted.

I remember the taste of my saliva. The bitterness. The acidity. Just opening the door had transferred something from inside the cabin to inside my body. Smell is the most difficult of the senses to convey or erase. Above all, I remember that this thing I was unable to identify irritated my throat, my larynx, my esophagus, making me want to vomit.

"We were suspicious when the wolf began to prowl," the man translated again, slowly, looking at her instead of me, trying to confirm that he was translating correctly. "When it prowled outside the door."

"Is that normal here?" I asked him directly, already knowing the answer.

The translator looked at me, distraught. Was that fear in his voice? Or in his eyes, or in the way he placed his hands over the illuminated part of the table?

"If this is true," he said, "they will never tell us anything."

"It was actually a wolf cub," interrupted the girl, as the translator quickly translated.

"Does that change anything?" I said immediately, without realizing that the young woman was still talking. "Is this detail important?" I asked again.

With a flick of his wrist, the man indicated that I should keep quiet. The woman was saying something. She was still saying something—something the man seemed incapable of believing, or even understanding. His mouth slightly open. His questions bumping into each other, one after the next. His hands raised. Whatever he was hearing was upsetting the usual slow, cautious rhythm of his translating.

That the wolf cub had arrived one morning and planted itself at the cabin door as if it were the most natural thing to do, is what the translator said later, when the young woman with blond hair had left and we were lying on the goose feather mattress, unable to sleep. That it didn't let anyone near the cabin. That it circled around as if the circle its paws made over the earth and eventually over the snow would serve as a shield and protect them from something that came from the forest. That when the wolf rested it licked, one by one, its paws.

"And this," I raised myself onto my right elbow to ask. "This is important? This explains why they are not here or where they went?"

"I don't know," the translator said, lying on his back on the mattress, his body tucked inside his sleeping bag, staring up at the ceiling. "I suppose that if it weren't related," he reflected, "she wouldn't have mentioned it."

Then, as if there were nothing left to say and he was suddenly alone, he placed small headphones over his ears. All I was able to hear of the music were tribal drums and screams. Soft screams, if there can be such a thing. Screams that multiplied, one after the other, yet remained unchanged.

IX: There Is a Waterwheel Outside

That the mission, seeming so simple at the beginning, had become complicated is what I would write in my report for the man who was waiting for news on the other side of the ocean. Was he forgetting to brush his teeth? Was he biting his nails from time to time? Was he wearing mismatched socks? Surely he was. Waiting is a very difficult task, a thankless task. Nervous. When I thought of him, which wasn't very often, I imagined him nervous, pacing around his office or his bedroom in silence. The silence of useless words. That I couldn't bring the woman home because she had already left, perhaps long before I came to the house on the edge of the Taiga, I would have to tell him at some point. That I still didn't know the date of my return. That return was not possible.

I remember the immobility. I remember thinking "but the sun never shines here," and the initial frustration too. And the deep breath I needed in order to sit up on the horrendous nauseating mattress, which I could only stand when I was inside my sleeping bag: the creaking of my knees, the pain in my neck, and the smell, that ominous smell.

The translator opened the door.

"There is a waterwheel outside," he announced. The news surprised me. Immediately I imagined a vertical tunnel that bore into the earth, earth that eventually transformed into pure ice. I didn't respond because I thought I had misunderstood. I was quiet because I assumed that at some point he would correct himself. The icy wind blew through his hair and mine. Then, without saying another word, the translator opened a thermos and offered me hot water from its cap.

"Where did you get it?" I asked. It was the first time I saw him smile. Without saying anything else, he took a small bag of tea from the pocket of his backpack and placed it in the steaming liquid. When I reached for the cap, I noticed that my hand was trembling.

"You aren't used to this cold, are you?" he murmured. "Or these dark trees," he continued without waiting for my response.

I told him the truth. I told him no, I wasn't.

In fairy tales, the wolf is always ferocious. Astute and agile, the wolf always figures out how to get its way. In the most watered down versions of Little Red Riding Hood, the wolf is killed by the woodsman, and in others by the wisdom and strength of the grandmother herself. In the original version, the figure of the wolf is used to convey strict moral lessons. The wolf, in other words, always wins. Lying in the grandmother's bed, wearing her nightgown and even her sleeping cap, the wolf waits for the girl in order to see her better, touch her better, bite her better: consume her. In the oldest versions, the wolf not only wins, but wins in the most atrocious way. Lying in the grandmother's bed, perhaps without any clothes on at all, the wolf invites the little girl in the red hood to eat the meat and drink the blood of the old woman. In a time besieged by hunger and scarcity, who could resist such an invitation? Little girls shouldn't go into the forest and, if they find themselves in the forest, little girls shouldn't talk to strangers. No, no, and no. Not little girls.

While we drank hot tea by the waterwheel behind the cabin, we had to face the truth: We had no idea how to continue or where we were going. Discovering that this house had been watched or guarded by a small wolf that licked its paws had not helped us, not at all. A preliminary inspection of the dark interior of the cabin had also revealed very little: a few household tools, a pencil without lead or eraser, a dirty cotton shirt. Sometimes, frustration makes us look at the sky. At other times, it leads us to the waterwheel. What was a waterwheel doing in the middle of nowhere surrounded by trees? I screamed into it, the earth. One of those soft screams I had heard when I was lying close to the translator's headphones. Sometimes a scream turns into a song. He, as if infected, did the same. From the perspective of the woman slowly approaching with a basket, the scene must have seemed hysterical, to say the least. Here were two strangers on tiptoes, screaming into a waterwheel. An echo. Echoes. Here were those two, us two, insane.

"It's bread," the man said, translating the words of the woman with the slanted eyes, offering it to me.

"Ask her," I requested as I took the bread, still warm, and put it in my mouth. "Ask her."

When he did, when he spoke to her in her own language, the woman only lowered her eyes, a timid smile on her lips. She shook her head no. Not her, and shrugged her shoulders. Was that a hint of pink on her cheeks? That she couldn't speak about it, she seemed to have added before turning and disappearing down the path that led back to the village.

The translator, who watched me watching her, placed his headphones over my ears.

"Listen to this," he either said or ordered.

I remember the breadcrumbs on my molars. The way the taste swept through my mouth before arriving at the back of my tongue. Yeast. I remember the flock of black birds descending, swiftly, from somewhere in the sky.

X: Dance Theory

That, with time, I had become accustomed to the hollow moments of an investigation is true. There are hours, days even, sometimes months or years when nothing happens: Those are the gaps in an investigation. In other words, those moments are life. The detective who wins a case, who solves it, is usually the one who weathers those lapses. Resources are needed, of course. But above all, you need patience, that rare gift; or you need something else to think about—a certain capacity for distraction. You need a place inside the self, your own language where you can hide. You need a refuge, yes. Any refuge.

I remember the X-ray of a skull. I remember how the image appeared out of nowhere, suspended, wobbling, in front of my eyes. What if we saw everything through that film of black and gray and white? The picture showed that the skull, a cave of bones, looked strong enough to offer refuge. There, a body or the image of a body could curl up comfortably.

So this was where the woman had lived, the woman and the man. The second wife and this other man—of whom I knew nothing save that he was younger than her and knew how to dance—had lived here, from around the start of winter to the middle of summer. So this was the place. All those months, I whispered as I touched the walls, the surface of the table, the steel and pewter spoons. None of these objects told any secrets. So this was where she had caressed him, in this space: on this bed. Here, their legs and arms. Here, their hair, perhaps tangled. Their sweat? Here, no doubt, their sweat. They must have talked. They must have carried water from the waterwheel, for drinking or washing—it doesn't matter. They must have looked many times at the ice down below, at the end of the tunnel. When they had to relieve themselves, they must have walked together to the latrine and, after shutting the door, lowered their pants or leggings, the back part of their thighs touching the cold wooden surface. The smell of excrement. Black flies. They must have used the water from the waterwheel to clean off the remnants of fecal matter. The foul stench. So here was where.

Had she imagined all this, the second wife, when she accepted the hand offered her in the rancid smoky air of a dance floor? When her fingers met his, in that moment had she seen the forest and the shack, the waterwheel and the latrine? The truth is no one knows when they are making their biggest or most significant decisions. No one understands their own decisions. The woman danced with him; this was what the man from the coast had told me, in a café surrounded by windows that opened to the ocean.

I remember the salt. I remember the linen curtains that gave shape to the ocean wind. Someone said that when we open windows wide, the salt helps us remember who we are. Or how.

They had danced, yes. Together. In sync. They had moved toward the dance floor, to music manufactured by various synthesizers and computers. The sounds drowning out everything else. The sweat. The sweat again. The murmurs.

They had soared, delicately moving their necks, wrists, and hips. Their arms held high, hands swaying. Their spines responding first, almost subconsciously, to the beat, and only after to the melody. They had moved their lips then, repeating the chorus: words, whole phrases. Had he taken her by the elbow to move her from the dance floor to a terrace? Surely not. They must have danced until the end of the set. Smiling. Distracted. Sweaty. And when everyone else returned to their spots or prepared to leave, they must have found themselves, frozen and surprised, powerless to say goodbye. Looking at each other. Is that a nervous laugh? Yes, indeed. And that's a pair of knees.

Just outside the cabin, inspecting the surroundings, I walked from the waterwheel to the front door and from the front door to the latrine. The only thing I discovered was a few thin, short strands of hair. The blood I had seen in my mind, in the image of a pouncing wolf, shone in its absence. Buried bones. Pieces of flesh from some grandmother torn apart. All of this either wasn't there or didn't exist. Nothing hidden in the shed was worth anything either. If we hadn't been looking for them, if we hadn't followed their tracks from such a distance, nothing here would have reflected their presence. To seek something out is to expose it. I'd begun to question their presence on that morning of hot tea and screams into the waterwheel. Yes, I began to question if those two had really been here, if we weren't just inventing them.

The translator was the one who found the piece of paper with the pencil sketches. He was the one who brought it, overjoyed but keeping it to himself until he was back at the cabin. A child had given it to him, he said handing it to me. The child had said he had seen something in the house. This house. Twelve or thirteen figurines of flesh and bone. Twelve or thirteen little dolls covered in something that could have been placenta or blood. Twelve or thirteen things with voices and arms and necks. As if they were alive. As if they could die.

In what moment had the couple realized that they couldn't go back? I asked myself, still holding the paper in my hand.

XI: The Pool

There was a pool in the village, we discovered on our second day. Under the evening storm clouds, at once static and threatening, there was a pool. Yes, a rectangle. A blue rectangle surrounded by a garden. A blue rectangle with its still green lawn and children's games and patio tables and umbrellas. And behind, crowning everything, conifers. So many needles. And branches. A photograph from the glossy pages of a design magazine.

A pool in the middle of the Taiga? Yes, indeed, a pool in the middle of the Taiga. Yes.

The pool belonged to an older man who supervised the local lumber industry. It was terrifying to see it through the large windows of his living room: a blue pool with countless golden leaves scattered on its motionless surface. A diving board. Two iron ladders attached to each side of an underground wall. As I sat there, verifying that the leather of the giant easy chairs was indeed caribou,

I asked myself again and again, what was in the eyes of the second wife when she saw all this? What simmered there? How many birds in the palms of her hands? What was under the soft skin of her eyelids? She must have thought, just as I did in that exact moment, of her journal, of the pages where she had written about her desire. She must have thought of the pool and how she wrote the word "pool" on pages that were so fragile, so very small. She must have imagined the passage of time, the sudden change in seasons and of course the rectangle of ice that would soon take root inside her. So, this was it. So, my dear, this was what it was all about.

A blue pool: empty.

That the man in charge of the local lumber industry wanted to understand, I would write in the report I would eventually send to the man who paced nervously in his bedroom, in his head. The most powerful man of the region was curious. What exactly had brought us from a place that he imagined was so distant, maybe even the most distant, to this corner of the world, a corner he considered (and in the strictest sense he was correct) his own? He offered us tea. Then he offered us vodka. Between one thing and the next, a slight woman with almond eyes and long straight hair brought us bread and sea salt and small sprigs of something that looked like parsley but could just as easily have been dried seaweed. Then she served, on a large platter, hunks of meat that our host ate with his fingers, motioning us to do the same.

I remember the movement of jaws, constant and dreadful. Opening and closing. Chewing. Swallowing. I remember how the voracity of my own chewing made me close my eyes. Sometimes pleasure is like that. Above all, I remember the sound of lips, gnawing and talking at the same time, and the grease shining on those lips. And how my food slid down my esophagus, slowly, before falling into the cruel mechanism of my stomach. All those liquids. All that acid. I remember the noise of gold chains around forearms and wrists. How the metal sparkled at that time of day. What time? What day?

He wanted to know if we were looking for the little girl, that's what he said. For the little girl and the boy. And the translator, who was peering through the windows with the same determination that I was, told him yes, we were. We were looking for a girl, yes, and a boy. Two people who, as we understood it, were lost in the Taiga. Of course, he must know about the syndrome? The man's laugh certainly surprised us. A loud guffaw. How the noisy laughter crashed against the glass of the large windows in the back of his house. Something split in two, into so many more.

"But you are too late, right?" the translator told me the older man had asked, still eating, swallowing, muffling his words. Still drinking. Snorting.

I remember the fear again, the sensation. That someone was watching us, I felt certain. The gaze fell, sharply, over my right shoulder, at first just the prick of an arrow, but then something much larger. Some kind of cold compress. An injury, yes, and its cure. Both at the same time. When I told the translator to ask the man how he had electricity there, inside and even around his house, the man pointed to a small wooden room at the far end of the back garden: a private converter. I scrutinized the corners of the room that we were in: no video cameras.

I examined the lamps, the edges of the table, the fringes of the curtains. It was something else, no doubt. Something coming from outside, from beyond the window. Something.

Hours later, when the translator and I were already inside our respective sleeping bags, lying on the filthy mattress, he would whisper to me, as if someone or something could hear us, that the man had been suspicious of them, of this pair of children who suddenly appeared out of nowhere. He had believed and perhaps still believed they were spies—from the central government or some foreign competitor, it was all the same to him. Agents from large corporations trying to come and re-establish order, or worse, create a new order. He had sent for them to make sure they were not spies, or if they were, to make sure they stopped.

"But they weren't spies, were they?" the translator would ask me, propping himself up on his left elbow. His small face, with its almost feminine features, was just above mine. His smooth youthful skin. His constant blinking. And when he asked that, resting there on his elbow, his face so close to mine, I couldn't stop myself from laughing.

"So you think we're in an action movie?" I asked him, trying to suppress a disruptive laugh, even placing my hand over my open mouth.

Then the man put on his headphones again and closed his eyes, pretending to sleep. But before actually doing so, before falling into a private refuge protected by the hard hollow bone of his skull, he sat up once more.

"He didn't want to talk about the pool," he said. "When I asked him, he wouldn't say anything about it. Did you see how he looked at it?" he asked me before falling onto his back.

I told him the truth. I told him yes.

I remember the child I imagined when I looked at the businessman. When I looked at him out of the corner of my eye all I saw was a boy—a monster more than a child in the strictest sense of the word. Something eager in the open mouth. The rows of sharp teeth. The chubby hands. Some sort of giant lumbering fool, the sight of whom caused more disgust than terror. The verb "to inundate."

The presence of the word "saliva": something sticky and dirty and discarded. Something difficult to escape. Power always produces these kinds of sensations.

"Do you think the man has something to do with their disappearance?" I asked him, truly intrigued by the possibility. But by that time the translator was already lying on his back, his headphones over his ears, unable to respond.

I remember the images from my dream. I remember it was in my dream that I saw the small hand, its shadow on the wooden wall. A hand as small as the head of a pin. How many angels were dancing, deranged, on the tip of its nail? A hand that could have easily passed for the corpse of a mosquito or flea: a hand with five fingers, even tinier.

XII: Those Things

That I would have liked to be a housewife, I sometimes thought, even a slightly sad housewife. Instead of wandering around faraway lands, trying to answer impossible questions, there were times (knowing this was improbable) I would have preferred to be a housewife. But I wasn't and never had been, and never would be. Instead, I was a person who walked over lots of sharp stones asking if anyone had seen something odd, a hand, maybe a very little hand to be more exact, on a wall, or on the wall of a dream. I might be a person who shivered but I could take the cold.

The little boy emerged from the same path used by the woman with the basket of bread and the young woman in the wool hat. We heard steps, and when the sound of feet over loose earth was just a few yards away, we opened the door. The sound of creaking. The truth is I had expected to see an adult. The diminutive figure, the look of fear, or rather terror, in his eyes opened immeasurably wide, disappointed me. But the translator invited him in.

"And your mother?" he asked, or told me he had asked him.

"Over there." The boy pointed out an indeterminate place in the village that I had begun to refer to as "the zone." His finger raised.

"You made these?" the translator pressed, pulling out wrinkled papers from a pocket in his backpack.

He, the boy, told the truth. He said yes.

"Why?"

"Because I saw it."

"Where?"

"Here."

No one needed to translate this exchange for me.

"But it's not real," the translator said, shaking his head, attempting a smile.

"Yes it is," the boy insisted without blinking. "It's here."

I remember the boundaries on the map I either saw or anticipated in that moment. Long ago, when cartography was just beginning—though it was already a matter of life or death, and not just for those who went to sea—maps were called "Portolan charts." From some place in my mind the words "Carta Pisana" emerged. The date: 1290. The sophisticated outline of the shores. The details of life at the bottom of the enormous sea. Above all, I remember how, all at once, the whole forest closed in on us. I remember feeling suddenly small.

Like the blond woman from before, the boy sat at the table in front of the translator. This time, instead of taking my usual spot on the bed, I stood in the doorway. Sounds of birds all around me. The sound of something passing by. Sudden swaying. Branches. Leaves. I peered into the forest but whatever it had been had already left. Only air. Air in motion. If the child had not really wanted to speak, he never would have come by himself, sneaking away from his mother, to the cabin on the edge of the village. Still, with his hands clasped and resting on the table, the boy scrutinized us. He seemed to know that inside himself he held a treasure, and as anxious as he was to share it, he also wanted to make sure it was worth something to his listeners. Why give someone a gift if they don't want it? For quite some time, I had asked myself that same question. Yes.

Hours later, as we lay in bed again, each in our own sleeping bag, staring at the ceiling, the translator would tell me, his mouth still twisted in disbelief, what the boy had said.

Before that, before night fell, the translator had asked me to come with him to try and find provisions in the only commercial area in town. We needed clean water to drink and something to eat that wasn't caribou or reindeer. We needed soap and salt and perhaps sugar. Above all, we needed to see the faces and bodies of the people in this place, a place we'd traveled to thinking we would soon be leaving, thinking that we could. I walked by his side, using the same path our visitors had taken when they came to speak to us. I walked, I should specify, near him but not next to him, on account of his great speed, his absolute concentration on what was in front of and beyond us, his way of never looking back.

Above all, I remember the sound, sometimes desperate, sometimes ragged, of my breath. When I was a little girl, and the length of my legs made it impossible to maintain the rhythm and pace of adults, I would breathe like that. I remember it clearly. It wasn't the physical effort involved that mattered. What mattered, what made me so angry that it distorted my breath—that faint but efficient flow of air through the diaphragm, the bronchial tube, the lungs—was the emotional frustration. If they knew I couldn't keep up with them, why didn't they just slow down? So that I wouldn't walk with them? So that I had to ask them to walk slower? I remember looking toward the sky. The flight of the birds. Was that the sound of squirrels darting? The movement of something leaving.

That they had eaten the same thing as everyone else that day is what the boy said. For the very first time, a foreign couple had attended a community celebration. A ritual, no doubt. A way of fighting the scarcity of food that had led to the forest's exploitation, while also keeping community ties alive when people were facing the constant economic pounding involved in the production and exportation of lumber. Although they had been invited before, the couple had not accepted the invitation for reasons everyone thought strange and even suspicious. Spies, that is what they were, everyone knew this, or demons. But that day, the day he wanted to tell us about, something had happened. Definitely hunger. Maybe boredom. Something to make the time pass. They had eaten the same soup with vegetables, greens, and hunks of meat. The low flames licking the iron pot. The burning wood. They were served from the same metal spoon, used the same wooden bowls, were given the same food. But that night, unlike the others, unlike the locals, the woman had vomited.

They had already been lying down when it happened. The woman had doubled over and without knowing why touched her stomach and then her forehead. Sweat maybe. Fever. Without waking the man, she circled the bed a few times, and, once outside, the cabin. Barefoot. She would have discovered him, the boy said, if she hadn't been devoting her attention, all her attention, to the condition that was making her double over with nausea. It would have been easy to spot him, standing by the window, peeking through a crack.

I remember the passage of the light. The word: "filter." The word: "wedge." Above all, I remember that everything we see, we see through a crack. I remember, right now, how it saves us.

How the woman had vomited. On the bed, beside the man's body. How, from that vomit, from that jumble of bones and saliva and bile, from that truly nauseating smell, from that unbearable substance, those things had appeared. Those things the boy had drawn later, much later, at the request of the translator. On a sunny morning. A spectacular morning.

XIII: *L'Enfant sauvage*

That lumberjacks can be cautious I knew, or sensed: either way it doesn't matter. Their proximity to sharp-toothed heavy tools must have something to do with it. Occupational hazards. Their close relationship, so paradoxical, almost organic, with the forest they kill and that sustains them. Do these thoughts pass through the mind of a lumberjack as he saws and cleaves and hacks at the tree bark? During those days, I asked myself that question frequently. And I answered: They think all this and more. Or they would.

It was the lumberjacks who walked along the edge of the cabin carrying him. It was they who led him— "dragged him" would be more accurate—to the central market where just the day before the translator and I had found salt, a little black tea, sugar, three or four potatoes. Some utensils. A pewter plate. Two cups.

· · ·

In the movie *L'Enfant sauvage*, directed by François Truffaut in 1970, the hunters were unable to capture the wild child—or, to be more precise, the feral teenager—from the trees where he would swing and leap; they only managed it after they forced him into a hole. The dogs' pursuit drove him to seek refuge underground, and in the end, it was the smoke from a burning log that did the trick. Coughing, forced into a sack, resisting his new condition, the child was taken to a small village from which, a few days later, thanks to the interest of a budding psychiatrist, he would be transported to a large capital city. Between one place and the next, when he was still in the public space of the first city he was brought to, the feral child was presented in a kind of improvised parade where he bit other children and ran every which way. His hair tangled. His face dirty, his expressions of wrath and disgust. But disconnected from anything human. Before, shortly before, when he was still locked in a barn, his feet bound, the boy managed to break the glass of a window. This is what I wanted to get at, the moment when this peculiar romance is established between the feral child, the window, and the spectator.

...

I remember the light through the many windows. Memory dangles these windows in front of me, at daybreak, just barely covered by a thin linen curtain. Then the same windows in the middle of the day, opened wide. The windows again in the evening, and above all, I remember the hands on them, all over the glass. And the nostalgia of this, of what's on the other side, the great beyond, as it used to be called. Above all, I remember I used to exhale in front of them, in front of the glass, and write with the tip of my index finger the words "I am leaving this place" and "I will never return."

What I saw in front of me, what was beside me, almost within reach, in the middle of a semicircle formed by people, curiosity, and terror, could only really be seen through this window. Sometimes a rectangle is a sacred shape. Months later, in the vast metropolis, the feral child would look through this window with great nostalgia. And he would do it again and again. And then, one more time. Looking. Imagining that he could return, the wild child of the boreal forest who rattled the chain that bound his left shin to a wooden post, who without a doubt saw us as well, through the window. But what and how did he really see? The rectangle is often a sacred shape. He calmed down when he realized he couldn't break the chain. He leaned back on the post and observed us. He did this for a long time. Exhausted. First cautiously and then, later, his breathing steadied, with total insolence. Looking straight ahead. With compassion as dark as it was direct.

I remember the bird's eyes. Above all, I remember the question the woman wrote so often in her journal about whether the bird could see her through the windows. I remember the miniscule handwriting, page after page, asking this question. I remember the light in those eyes. The speed.

He wasn't really a child in the strictest sense of the word, more of a teenager. He had long locks, and curly body hair covering his forearms, his legs, his chest, his back, his genitalia. His mouth was wide. His hands, surprisingly delicate. Before long, a woman placed a blanket over his shoulders. Before long, someone approached him with a cup of hot water. Then, the voices: how many more times? When would he stay away for good? It became clear that this had happened before: caught, forced to stay, let go. That is what the lumberjacks and the inhabitants of the region said. It was always the same. His long arms. His protruding ribs. Get out of here already.

That he lived in the forest, but not too deep inside, is what I would write in my report for the man from a city that was becoming increasingly difficult to imagine. Or rather, that he hung around. The feral boy from the Taiga let himself be caught on a regular basis, especially toward the end of autumn and the beginning of winter when the temperatures began to drop drastically or when he was sick or when some sprain made it difficult to climb trees or leap to the highest branches. In those cases, they would let him spend the night on a pile of furs in some shack, or would even leave him a couple of boiled potatoes, bones with meat clinging to them, in the places they knew he frequented. Just in case. But then, still fearing him, maintaining a distance, unable to watch him constantly—he would disappear again. He would leave. His scratches would leave as well, his tangled hair, his incapacity to speak. He would leave without anyone realizing. What had happened some months before, however, was unusual.

Without ever asking anything but by listening to the voices of the crowd that gathered around him, the translator could deduce that the adolescent of the boreal forest had acted more or less like the wolf cub outside the couple's cabin door. Not that they would have been able to see him. No. But in those days and months, while the man and woman were there, inside, making strange noises and emitting groans similar to the noises of wild animals, they had noticed small thefts of food and a peculiar movement in the tree branches nearby. Something going by swiftly. Something spying from not very far away. It was difficult to know what he was looking for or what he wanted or from what danger he was protecting them.

A ferocious wolf; a feral child. I thought about the pair those two made outside a cabin.

I watched him, like the others, among the others, for a long time. I saw him beside the boy who spied through a crack in the window and beside the woman with short blond hair and so close to the other with almond-shaped eyes who had given us the bread. I had no idea who the others were. But my morbid fascination thrilled me. Who can resist observing the original body? A body without a social context? And as the minutes passed, I was also excited, no doubt, by my own incomprehension. I could never understand something like this, I told myself several times. I said it exactly like that: "I could never understand something like this." But I couldn't stop looking at him, fascinated, perhaps even bewitched or hypnotized by his thin figure, his exhaustion. Did he see me then, not by looking but by chance, not by directing his gaze my way intentionally but by letting his eyes clumsily meet mine? Something like that, yes. An arrow plunged into the left shoulder. A hole. And suddenly that moment produced the window. And the window produced the spectator. And those three elements together made the romance real. The passion. Someone longed for a freedom that was really an infernal abyss. Someone placed hands, now motionless, on the window. Someone who wanted to escape but couldn't escape and could only watch.

XIV: Placenta

That something burst out of her mouth, with or passing through the vomit, was clear from the translator's summary of the boy's words. It was only little by little that those two had admitted something was moving on the bed. Something lifted its head, twelve or thirteen times. Something extended scrawny arms and tiny legs. Maybe fifteen or eighteen centimeters tall? Fifteen or eighteen centimeters, yes. And as that thing moved, slowly and painstakingly, ridding itself of the saliva or placenta, they looked at each other. The man and the woman, barely dressed. Her mouth open and on her lips his tongue, his mouth. Also his fingers. Searching. For what? Exploring deep inside. "To probe" is a verb.

That it is difficult to translate the words for sexual body parts, especially with a small child, that this all could be the result of such a difficulty or of the imagination—either the child's or the translator's—I would have to make clear before continuing with the report that I would eventually write for a man who may or may not have existed.

That the word "frenzy." Him toward her, horizontally. Her toward him, vertically. Arms entangled. One mouth inside another, hands, nails. This is the noise that originates in the animal kingdom. This is its smell. There is a window that looks through me. His head seeking—what?—between her legs. Something that bites or strangles. That the man mounted her, atop her breasts, both of his knees on her shoulders, and placing his hand on her right cheek he coaxed her to keep her head angled and still. That once there he again put his thing into her mouth, that *thing*, that was what the child called it. Immediately, in the middle of the story, the translator had chosen to use the words "genitals," surely to avoid confusion between those things—that is to say, the tiny creatures, and his thing, in other words, the man's penis. While this was happening, the man kept his hand on the naked ass of the woman. Certainly seeing everything through a crack in a window made it difficult to distinguish what belonged to whom or what was really what. But that the movements of the man increased in speed and the stillness of the woman became absolute. Her mouth. Her ribs. That in the frenzy, in the middle of so many fluids and noises, they could not have been aware of when or how it happened.

That he had pulled her to him, flipping onto his back. And, moving together now, with the woman on top of him and him inside her, they began to hear the cries. When he got up from the mattress, when he was finally able to sit, he brought his hand to the back of his torso. And there, with both tenderness and disgust, he detached from his body two or three or maybe more tiny creatures. The blood from the vomit that could have been the blood of childbirth mixed now with the blood of death. Saliva. Excrement or tears, it doesn't matter. Broken bones.

Had all this really happened? Impossible to know for sure. Children are untrustworthy informants. The linguistic abilities of a translator are never perfect, or at least they weren't in this case. And then of course there was the question of my hearing—impressionable to say the least—right after having seen, through the window of reality, the other boy in the forest. The desire between one thing and another. The desire of bodies and, at the same time, the desire to narrate bodies.

"But you know this isn't real, right?" the translator stressed when the child finished his story.

"Yes it is," the boy insisted, without blinking, staring straight at him. "Here."

I remember his small hands, one inside the other. A little later: his entwined fingers. His broken and dirty nails. His cheeks, red, more from the cold than the sun. Above all, I remember the question: Why did I think that all of this would lead to finding a woman in a faraway place and saying to her, "Come back"? I remember how I ran my fingers through the child's hair, how I rested my hands for a few seconds on the back of his shoulders before turning around and leaving, one more time, out the door that opened onto the forest. I raised my face and breathed deeply. A village where the children peek through cracks in the windows. I made my way cautiously through the trees. The sound of my steps over the dry branches kept me alert. I touched the bark of the trees, broke off a few pieces without really realizing it. Sometimes desperation makes us put things in our mouths. Sometimes it is boredom. I did it: I tasted it. The Taiga on my wisdom teeth combined with my saliva. I swallowed it. I remember the house with all the lights on, which I saw as I turned to look behind me. I remember that, just in that moment, it began to snow again.

XV: Lap Dance

That we needed to do something, something different, is what I said to the translator on our third night in the cabin. I already wanted to leave. I cared little or not at all about the woman, or the man, or what had happened here. I repeated the word "here," a little scornfully, frustrated. The report, which I continued writing, little by little, in a code that in the end only I would be able to understand, didn't contain much of a case. Nothing at all, really. Just a husband pacing in a room or in his head while the world outside kept spinning. Just a man who doesn't understand, I insisted, as if that explained everything. The translator, who was listening to me carefully, without moving a single muscle in his face, let out a loud laugh.

"And what did you think?" he asked, rummaging around his backpack, barely raising his eyes, "That someone would come this far and not be leaving for good?"

. . .

I remember the river, the dark water of a river where I washed my feet. I remember its shores and the sound of its water, flowing. Why do we remember things like that? The strange feeling that something under the water, under the swirling water, would bite or injure or claw us. The uncomfortable sensation of bare feet on shifting ground. But was this a river or the ocean? The gray of the sky blended into the water.

"I thought that a person who sent messages from everywhere they went would be the sort of person who wanted to be found," I said, hesitating. "That's what I thought."

The translator rubbed his lips together, closed his backpack, tightened the laces of his boots, and stretched out his hand.

"Come," he said.

Instead of walking on the path our visitors had used, we took the path that led toward the forest. Into the forest. Under its branches. Above its dry leaves. Surrounded by the sound of owls beginning to stir. Nearby their astonishing eyes and the beating of their wings. How many of them were there? I wanted to stop to see if I could see the sky but I was afraid that the translator, who rarely looked behind him, would keep going. Besides, in the end, what could be so special about a sky that was as dark as the forest we were walking through? Following this route, it didn't take long to get to the village and, once on its dirt roads, to find the door the translator was seeking. Past the door there was another door, and then a curtain. We only stopped after the curtain hit the floor behind us.

Places where sex is sold are the same everywhere. They always have a viewing window or something similar: a bar, a walkway, a stage where you can see bodies and, if permitted, feel them. It has to be a space that facilitates the circulation of these bodies, so that they can be appraised, touched, negotiated. And it must have an area in which to complete—once agreed upon, once contracted—sexual intercourse. The noise of people or glasses or music always helps. Smoke. Something unspeakable in the air. All of this was present in the place the translator had taken me. We sat in front of a small bar and ordered drinks. With the drinks in hand we headed to another bar in the shape of a semicircle, where a couple of women with large breasts, having apparently recently given birth, were letting the patrons suck on their nipples and extract breast milk. Another woman was stripping on a small table and, after bending over to better display her ass and anus, she sat on the lap of two or three lumberjacks waiting for her. Copulating, right there, on the red plastic seat, back to chest, laughing the whole time. Soon, the translator grabbed me by the hand and led me through the noise and the people and the smoke.

"But what if this place goes on forever," I said, laughing, a little dizzy from the noise, from the presence of so many bodies close together, from two drinks. And he, as usual, continued ahead without looking back.

To pass through an even smaller door he had to lift two heavy red velvet curtains. Once inside, the noise of laughter and glasses and music ceased. The multitude of clients shrank to a couple of groups of men and women dressed in elegant neat clothes. Some were even speaking the language the translator and I spoke to each other.

"What are we waiting for?" I asked after a few minutes, when I realized that nothing was happening where we were. My murmur mixed with so many others. The anticipation, clearly, was shared.

"I don't really know," the translator said, disappointed. "One of the women in the village assured me that what we were looking for was here."

We took a seat not far from the main bar, where the mirror, wide and beveled, reflected our image: two adults adrift in a·sumptuous gilded cave. An excess of red. An excess of smoke. If someone had seen us from far away they would have thought that we were older than we really were, or perhaps that we suffered from a respiratory disease that forced us to open our mouths in order to breathe. It was then that I realized how much my hair had grown; it was arranged in a braid that, according to the mirror, fell a little below my shoulders. How long since I had looked at myself like this? And it was also then that I realized the strange beauty of my guide: his short straight hair, his round skull, his strong jaw. A man and a woman pursuing another man and woman. So, will everything end here? I asked myself silently, vainly observing the wrinkles that the mirror of the bar showed me. The exhaustion, the countless age spots. Will everything end, after all this, in a common brothel? With a lap dance? I looked up at the crystal chandelier hanging from the ceiling. I distracted myself counting its gleaming edges. I laughed mirthlessly.

Like the translator, I wasn't sure what we were waiting for, but unlike him I was already bored with the outcome. After all, for nearly an eternity destitute women have come to places like this, either to survive hostile conditions or hoping to find a means to escape. I had, in fact, come prepared for just such a possibility. I had made a promise, I remembered in that moment. I had money in a little hidden pocket of my pants. I had promised to bring back a woman.

I remember the wolf's leap. The way his hind legs slowly peeled away from the snow while his front legs, suspended in the air, seemed to reach out for something more. I remember that I saw, right in that moment, the image again. A large fully grown wolf; a wolf with thick fur, leaping toward something I couldn't yet discern, but that without a doubt was there, in the next image. Below, the red thread continued to unwind and, upon hitting the trunk of that same majestic fir tree, ascended to the heavens.

Suddenly, the voice of a woman overwhelmed everything, scraping the walls of the entire place. One or two sounds at the same time, both from one throat. Was that possible? Yes, it was possible: the syncopated rhythm of a brook, the gallop of a mare, the song of certain birds. Even the color green, yes. A stone as it's rolling. When a waiter in a dark formal coat came into the room with the red velvet curtains carrying a tray in his gloved hands, I thought, perhaps like the others, that it was caviar. I should have suspected something when, placing it on a long shiny bar made from the tallest evergreens, he smiled with only the left half of his face. It wasn't this man but another in a black suit and gold-rimmed glasses who lifted the glass cover.

It is difficult to describe what is impossible to imagine.

The two miniature creatures seemed, at first glance, to be dolls. Maybe fifteen or eighteen centimeters tall? The type of dolls that certain little girls still play with. When they began moving, I instinctively looked above them for the strings by which, from some real though hidden place, a puppeteer was no doubt controlling them. A customer passing his hands horizontally over the dolls must have had the same idea, and had also arrived at the same conclusion: Their movement was, in fact, self-directed. Whether by will or desire, it didn't matter. I believed then that they were robots. I thought they must be the deranged creation of some lecherous man because, yes, these two miniature creatures with long hair and legs were in that moment tangled in an embrace that was certainly sexual. One, in fact, had mounted the other. The other, opening its companion's legs, entered her with hands and tongue. The one got on its hands and knees and raised its tiny ass. The other penetrated her with the help of instruments that would have seemed comical in any other context. One looked at us with real curiosity. The other looked at us with scorn. One moved its head toward the other and opening its lips pronounced words or emitted sounds that we couldn't hear. Their hands interlaced.

"How much did you pay to get in here?" I hadn't planned on asking the translator that, but out of all the questions that swirled around in my head, it was the first to come out of my mouth.

"Courtesy of a man with a pool," he said, not taking his eyes from the scene.

Then, without warning, the man in the black suit and gold glasses put the glass cover on the creatures again, ending the scene that had seemed as if it were going to go on forever. In unison, the audience let out a groan of disappointment. A man held a wad of bills in the air to ask for more. There was nervous laughter. Sighs of disbelief. A woman leaned over the lid to see more clearly. The creatures, with their hands against the glass, looked at us. "Rosy-cheeked" is a celestial adjective. Even I yearned to insert my enormous ring finger into the pink between their legs. Even I wanted to fuck them or kiss them. Then, the voice materialized again. One or two sounds but from only one throat. A tableau vivant.

"That's enough," the translator said, indicating that it was time to leave. A robot lets itself be led, sometimes, just as I let myself be led in that moment. The same route in reverse. The images, returning. The intertwined hands.

"Lumberjacks are very strange men," I managed to say after we had been walking through the forest for a while, dumbfounded. The noises of elks and owls. And something that moves inside: silence or fear. A leaf falling. I asked myself many times during that journey: Who had dropped the radioactive crumbs shining around our feet?

XVI: Women Think Only about Sex

"What was in his semen, I wondered for the first time"—I would write in the report I prepared for the man who lived, if indeed he lived, far away. There must have been something in his semen, or in her eggs, or in the genetic material of both of their bodies, to produce those tiny creatures. When is it time to abandon a hallucination? Without a doubt when we start to act as if it is real or possible.

"It's terrible that he doesn't have a name," I said, looking up from the pad where I was writing my daily notes. "The wild child," I clarified, when the translator, who was once again fiddling with the numerous compartments of his backpack, looked at me, his brow furrowed, his mouth half open.

"Call him Victor," he said casually when he understood.

"Victor, yes," he repeated. And then without pausing he sat at the table, and moving the candle out of his way, said:

"They didn't go toward the city, they went into the forest, the boy insists that they went that way," and his face and hand moved in unison toward the northeast. "Do you still want to find them?"

"Her, yes," I said, remembering my promise.

"I figured," he said, turning to look at the bulky backpack lying by the door.

That on the morning of the fourth day, we set out very early. That I wouldn't bother to give him poetic descriptions of the beauty surrounding us: the flora, the fauna, the noises, the apparitions, the senses. It was enough to say that it was daunting and very difficult to keep moving ahead. He could easily understand this, I would write in the report that, despite my intentions, filled page after page of a small notebook with a black cover. The Taiga Syndrome. As for the translator—I would quickly and bluntly assure him that the translator stayed on, as did I, for the promise of more money. But what is money even worth in the middle of a boreal forest? A mere hallucination, I said to myself and to the tree that watched me leave.

We stopped several times to defecate and to eat. We drank hot water from the thermos and devoured, when necessary, the boiled potatoes the translator had had the foresight to pack. The forest's bounty. Its rhythm. It is difficult to transform garbage into a trail of crumbs. Urinating is a complicated operation, to say the least: the squatting, the exposure of unprotected flesh, the vapor that rises from the contact between the stream of urine and the cold rocks. We stopped to examine a strange artifact peeking out of the ground, alerting us to something else inexplicable: a plane's instrument panel full of buttons and levers that someone, at some point, must have lost control of. Heavily rusted. When I looked behind us, the world seemed incomprehensible and eternal. Time.

It is difficult to imagine what can't be described.

The forest, for others, is less uniform and less forest than it felt to me, judging by the paths we were crossing. The development of the timber industry had brought lumberjacks and businessmen alike. The needs of the lumberjacks had, in turn, brought cooks and merchants, usury and sex. In small rural houses, around fires burned down to embers, by heavy rust-colored machinery, men and women of different ages, covered by the same thermal coats, stretched and rested their muscles. From a distance they looked like small nomadic tribes. Off they went, carrying only what was needed for daily survival, tethered by ropes to a world that, though far from the forest, still tugged at them forcefully. Money is not a hallucination, I repeated to myself. The trees agreed with me. In the lumberjacks's pockets, in their gold teeth, in the chains that they wore around their necks, in their desire to leave forever, in their plans to return to some version of home that grew more remote the more they thought about it. Money shines with the patina of something sad or impossible. Something one should condemn.

"It's not a good life," the translator volunteered without my asking. "Too many drugs needed to keep up the work pace," he said, cutting off a piece of onion and bringing it to his mouth with the help of his pocketknife. "Too much, what is the word? Anxiety. Yes: too much anxiety."

I remained quiet so he would go on.

"I did it for several years before I went to college," he continued. "The pay is good, sometimes. It covered expenses." He stopped to spit. Then he looked toward the foliage and didn't say anything else for a while.

"It's impossible to live in those places for very long," he added, referring to cities. Too many people. Too much noise.

I remember his lips, their subtle movement. Above all, I remember the way they opened and closed, as if in slow motion. As if every word took years to form in some warm red region of his organs, only to emerge, at full speed, luscious, shaking itself off. I remember his cheeks, flaming red.

"Women think only about sex," he stated. And I, who had expected another comment that never came, laughed aloud without thinking. Because we were in the middle of a forest, sitting on the roots of trees that, after having grown for so many years, would be cut down without a second thought? I suppose this was why. What made me laugh, that is. For sure. Because no doubt Hansel and Gretel would have thought about it as well. Do all mothers and stepmothers and witches and lost girls think only about sex? Because the girl in the red hood must have thought about it relentlessly. Because of the lumberjack or lumberjacks. Because of the sale of bodies—of all bodies. Because the wolf, who had torn the grandmother to pieces and then worn her clothes, cross-dressing, taking the identity of one woman to attract another, had at some point certainly thought about it. But above all because the comment emerged out of the blue. A spontaneous artifact. And because, in the translator's subtle and tentative voice, from those thin dry lips that opened and closed in slow motion, there appeared, perhaps by accident, the sex of all of those women who, according to him, did nothing but think about sex, and by thinking about sex, thought of him.

"Do you think so?" I managed to ask him a while later, when my attack of laughter had subsided, even though I still had to wipe away the tears that had automatically sprung from my eyes and spilled over my cheeks. "Do you really think so?" I asked again without trying to stop the flow of mucous that poured from my nose and mixed, fluid and salty, with my tears.

"I do, yes," the translator insisted, his eyes staring at me in shock.

XVII: An Underwhelming Face

That we asked about them in every campsite we passed in the forest, I would write in the report that by now seemed more like an intimate diary than the kind of text that was meant to gather and provide precise and objective information. A summary of everything. The ultimate proof. That in all of the campsites there was always someone who had seen or heard of this mad couple of the Taiga followed closely by a medium-sized wolf and something else that wasn't human, hanging from the treetops. It was impossible not to sense that, with great difficulty, little by little, we were getting closer to our ultimate goal: to find her, talk to her, bring her back. It was impossible for us not to feel overcome by optimism. It wouldn't be the first time, after all, or the last. I would write that too, for the pure joy of it. For the optimism of it all.

We were getting close, that was clear. How difficult to walk when you have to pull your feet out of the mud. How difficult even to breathe, to keep breathing. Inhale. Exhale. Knees are a torture all their own. The last people we asked were a group of three moving through the forest in black overalls with gas masks over their faces. It was the translator who hurried to catch them, once we'd spotted them off in the distance: three figures at the end of the earth, their heads filled with clouds. Three survivors of a war yet to come. When they pointed their long metal canes at the makeshift tent—the tent which, though we did not yet know it, was our destination—we approached without fear. There was a small light inside: a candle maybe, or a kerosene lantern. Perhaps body heat, conversation. An army marching behind a white flag is what we were.

It's difficult to describe what can't be imagined.

Her face, for example. The woman's face. So underwhelming. Her hair, organized in two braids, fell behind her ears. Her freckles. The look in her eyes, always questioning. Where had she found the ribbons she used to tie, artlessly, the tips of her braids? When she peeked out of the opening in the tent's circular door, we understood immediately that we shouldn't ask anything. That it wouldn't be necessary.

Above all, I remember the wind. The way it tousled the long hair of a girl who no longer existed. Its howl. Its persistent howling. I remember, above all, how it pounded the windows of a house by the sea. The fear of seeing everything smashed into smithereens. The fear of having been left alone, in a room, forgotten on a slip of land that had been transformed, thanks to the vigorous wind, into an island, adrift. I remember how my hands trembled and how I covered my face with blankets in order not to see. Not to see anything.

"I've been looking for you," I said, addressing only her.

"I know," she said. "That's why we stopped," she added, looking at him and not at me. Looking at his shape emerging.

From out of the tent, a man appeared, the man whom I had barely considered. I had wondered about his semen, it's true, I had even thought about his ribonucleic and deoxyribonucleic acid, but I had never imagined, for instance, his face. The hands he now placed on the back of the woman's shoulders. His legs, so long. I assumed that, like all lumberjacks in the area, the man who accompanied the woman I had been searching for had no other choice than to grow out his beard until it covered his cheeks and chin and neck. I wondered: How long since they'd looked in a mirror? I thought about this while she, sitting on a rock, placed her hand, protective, on the back of the hand that rested on her right shoulder. So much time dancing together! I exclaimed to myself.

"You might have to consider going back." I lowered my eyes when I said it, suddenly embarrassed by the words I had just uttered.

The woman smiled in response, her eyelashes fluttering. The wind.

Although she was right in front of me, I saw her as if through a telescope or a microscope. An astronomical lens. Something tilted. So, she had somehow managed to create the forest and the paths of the forest that she'd imagined in the pages of her journal? She didn't seem like a strong-willed woman, but possibly she was. She didn't have the bold or brash attitude of those who manage to transform desires into reality, but if it's true that journals are full of desires, then this woman before me, leaning on the hard thighs of the man with whom she

had fled, right after she had stopped breathlessly, without knowing what to do, on a dance floor, had turned
those desires into a reality. Her desires. I was facing
someone—I told myself several times, just to remember
what was so obvious that it could become transparent
and pass unperceived—who had managed to transform
the world, at least what was around her, into the world of
her desires. A trembling image, something that gleams.
What is between imagining a forest and living in a forest? What brings together the writing of a forest with
the lived experience of a forest? I remember it perfectly:
There were four people in front of a tent surrounded by
the trees of a forest just before a storm. As if through
a telescope or microscope, their bodies. Their dry lips.
Her voice.

"You must have seen the three astronauts of the end
of the world," was what she said. I remained silent and
mentally repeated what I had just heard to convince myself that, in fact, the woman I had been seeking had said
that. Three astronauts. The end of the world. With absolute clarity.

I told her the truth. I told her yes.

"For an eternity, they have been saying that this will all end." She paused. Again she touched the back of the masculine hand resting on her shoulder. She turned and lifted her face to look at him. "And yet, they keep on going."

She fell silent. We all did. Except for the wind, we were all silent.

"But they are clearly insane," I both said and regretted saying at the same time. In real time.

Is this the end of falling out of love? I told myself, knowing that I wasn't asking a question. There was no one I could ask.

The wind. How it howls. This.

XVIII: I Would Be Stopped by the Dark

That there are long tresses of hair that can easily be described as flames, but certainly many others have already
hit on that. His wife, his second wife, did in fact have hair
like that: radiant like a wild burst of fire, something that
soared. "The strange thing isn't that she left," I would tell
him, writing with great precision, word by word. Bone by
bone. A lit match, its flame, also burns. "What was strange
was that she stayed with him so long."

Many days later, when we were finally face to face,
assessing each other without shame or loyalty, I asked
myself honestly if the translator had been right. Do
women really think only about sex? I would look again,
up and down, at the man from this coastal city. I noticed, like the first time, the protrusion bulging from the
center of his masculine throat, which so many people
call an Adam's apple. The hint of a beard. The gleam of
bright white teeth.

"I'm very tired," I would say. As always, telling him the truth.

And he would insist, of course, shaking the little book with the black cover high in the air before hurling it against the window, where something was observing us. The world. A tree.

"Do you think I am just going to accept this?" he would ask incredulously.

Hansel was there. Gretel was there.

At one point, there was a wolf.

Once upon a time there was. Or there would have been.

"No, I don't," I would say to him, calmly, telling him the truth once again. "Sometimes," I would want to continue, but I would be stopped by a blow. Or by the dark.

XIX: Cruelty Never Is

That as soon as they were outside the tent, the noises of the storm began—this I also would have included in the report. I had never heard thunder in a place so packed with trees. The booming of the sky made me tremble. The wing beats of birds with no names, that couldn't have names. The violently clashing branches. The heart of the forest suddenly seemed to beat rapidly. "Breathlessly" is an adverb with rhythm. We all looked up at the sky and in unison looked back at the things on Earth. There was a translator, a detective, a couple of fugitives. Once upon a time there was. We kept looking at each other like that for a while, motionless, terrified. As if the world were churning and, fearful that everything would turn upside down, that the heavens would abruptly vomit en masse, we had just begun to understand.

· · ·

I still remember the steps of the wolf. Prowling beside us. Above all, I now remember that we couldn't see it.

That they knew about us had been clear from the start. We didn't know exactly how much they knew or what they knew or how they had figured it out, but judging by the first response the woman had given me, it was obvious that they were aware of our search and even our objective. Rumors move effortlessly in small densely populated pockets of the forest world. Yet it was difficult to put into words, even for myself, the exact purpose of our mission: to find her, talk to her, bring her back.

"We were able to find you," I said only to her, "because of all these." I took out some of the telegrams and letters that the man from the coast had shown me some time ago, how long ago?

"Ah, those," she exclaimed, as if she had trouble recognizing them. She stretched out her right arm, touched the material with a certain animal tenderness. She dropped the papers on her lap and still touching the hand that lay on her right shoulder said:

"It's nice that the mail still works, isn't it?" The man agreed with her. Or at least he smiled.

"You wanted us to find you. Didn't you? You wanted us to come for you," I said, though really I was asking.

"Oh, no," she answered immediately, smiling, like him. "No."

Her voice, so soft. Her wide forehead. The way she shook her head so sweetly. She was silent. She raised her head to see the face of the man who lowered his gaze to find hers. The masculine hand on the lower edge of her jaw. Below, the submandibular glands, the submental ganglia. Underneath, the veins and facial arteries and stylohyoid muscles; the digastric and the upper portion of the sternocleidomastoid. On top of all this, the man's hand. On top of this, skin that stretched all around her neck. Pure, glorious anatomy.

"We wanted him to know that we were OK," she said, again looking at us. "We wanted him to know that we weren't in danger."

The plural. The singular. And again, the plural.

The translator glanced at me out of the corner of his eye. Then, without saying a word, he went back to scraping the forest floor with a dry stick. His face bent over the path, his shoulders. The wind, picking up. The smell of the storm.

"You should leave soon," she said looking at the sky again. Something there, in the treetops, moving. Something all around.

I moved my head from left to right several times. The reason, no doubt, was the stormy gray hue. The gray that announces the threat or danger right before, before what? I smiled like them, along with them.

"How did you get here?" For the first time I questioned him directly.

They shrugged their shoulders at the same time. They laughed again. Hansel and Gretel, I thought, the real ones. Hansel and Gretel might have had a smile that big, that convincing. Perhaps even that serene.

"You never know until you arrive," he explained, as if it were something that everyone knew. Was it a joke? No, it wasn't. I turned to look at the dense forest under the threat of a storm that never arrived.

And behind us, crumbs: traces.

"It's simply a matter of starting one day," he continued. "Taking the first step and then the second."

Was it just my imagination or were their voices no more than the voices of two missing children? That's what they sounded like. From their lips to our ears, the voices of two children.

"Do you recognize this?" I handed them the village boy's drawings.

They sought each other's eyes again, but this time the man squatted beside the woman. A swiftly automatic reaction. His arm a barricade, protecting her. Behind, there was surely a castle with high symmetrical towers crowned by two-toned flags. Inside, in front of a lit fire or near a corner that opened to the world by way of a window, the woman sobbing. The girl. The spy. The fairy godmother. Outside the man watched us reproachfully.

"It wasn't necessary," he said. "Cruelty never is."

I thought that at any moment he might start shouting but the only thing he did was this: stroke the woman's hair with the palm of his hand. Again and again. And then he placed his chin on her skull, the woman's skull. And he looked at us with something that could have been compassion or maybe simply detachment.

And the wolf, in that moment, shrank back.

XX: Something Died Here

That the translator had already told me, in the local airport where our small dilapidated plane had touched down
and from where I was expecting to leave at any moment,
how he had been born in a wild and crazy city, a metal
oil-drilling structure built over an enormous lake—that
I would end up including in my report as well. Who else
would be interested in this? I asked and answered myself
at the same time: me, of course. A place prepared for the
future, for what was to come, he'd said, smiling: apartment
building and offices, libraries and theaters, basketball and
tennis courts, soccer fields: all above the water. Even re-
fineries, over the water. Thinking about it more, maybe
this place was to blame for all the strange situations he
had faced throughout his life. That this place hadn't prepared him as much as set his course. Anyone born there
couldn't help but search, hopelessly, for something that
was either more incredible or more insufferable.

"But I thought you were from over there," I said, signaling the area he had pointed out to me before we left: the Taiga.

"Yes," he said. "Of course, from over there, exactly."

I assumed that I hadn't understood. And I assumed that it didn't really matter. It never had. I also assumed that the local authorities at the airport wouldn't care if a short man with large black eyes took sips from a small flask with me.

"To another failure," I said less for him, who wouldn't understand, and more for me, only for me really, before raising the flask and taking another swig.

I remember, above all, how we touched each other: in absolute peace. I remember how we had arrived, exhausted, at the cabin. The silence of disbelief. How fingers traced the edges of a mouth. Eyes opened wide. The pulsing of something in our wrists, in the pits of our stomachs, on the tips of our tongues. Does a heart beat inside the feet as well? I remember the storm that didn't come. I remember the tall treetops, their movement. The long walk. The moment when we said goodbye and turned our backs on it all. Our gradual detection of the crumbs.

"Something died here," I managed to say when we opened the door and the smell from the cabin hit us in the face again. Sometimes exhaustion can be confused with the urge to vomit.

The translator went out to get water from the waterwheel. Then, with an energy I lacked, he lit the stove. There he warmed his hands and there, his face illuminated, he must have thought about what he would say later.

"It has been fun," he murmured. "So much of it."

I remember it all, in the light of the fire. The sounds of the forest, surrounding us. How "to outline" is a verb. A finger traces a face, creating it. An arm behind a neck: supporting it. Above all, I remember that I had never slept in such stillness.

It was when dawn drew to a close that the lumberjacks appeared. Their footsteps, their torches. The stench of their alcohol. They walked now like before, like some other time. How long ago? A mob or a parade. The screams of a tribe, so loud. The banners. The flags. Sometimes birds pause like that, flush with the windows. And they look inside, terrified. But what, really, is the end of falling out of love? The men made a dreadful noise and then they left just as they had come. Abruptly. Their traces in the dark. Their shrieks: echoes.

It is never necessary, cruelty. Cruelty is.

When the translator opened the door, he stood silent for a long time. I was going to follow him but, with one hand raised, he said no. That I please not follow. For my own good. He then doubled over. I imagined this was because of the effort it took to carry the wild child—the weight of the body was more than he had expected. Those broken bones, that hair covered in semen and blood. Those hands. I assumed that the waterwheel. Everything falls at the same rate.

Cruelty, which is what it is.

I remember his shocking proximity. Afterwards. And that he gnashed his teeth ceaselessly. Death makes us want to put things into our mouths. I remember the tears on his expressionless face—the way he fell silent.

"WHAT ARE WE REALLY LETTING IN WHEN WE SAY GOOD-BYE?" The woman had written something like that in a telegram that she had sent from an outdated office of a small city near the Taiga.

The urgency of capital letters. That flock.

XXI: The Large Window that Vibrates

It wasn't until days later I realized I remembered something else. It was the image of her wings, a sound. The wings of the woman peering into a window. "And what do birds see?" she—not I—had asked herself, on one of the pages of her journal.

I returned to the coast on a very sunny morning. Instead of talking to the man who had hired me to find the woman who had fled to the Taiga, I spent time reviewing my correspondence, watering my plants, removing the spoiled food from the refrigerator. What happens to a house when it is abandoned is always unimaginable. The amount of dust and shadows. The quantity of messages on the answering machine. Garbage everywhere. Had that much time really passed? I was frightened. I didn't know how to look the man in the eye, to face that confused expression. He seemed lost—or was it resignation? Did he really think I would be returning with her in tow? I imagined he had known the answer from the beginning. And to think that he knew or had known only added to my questions about the origins of this case.

"Why did you really send me there?" I asked when he showed up without warning on my doorstep. I assumed that desperation, out of pure chance, had directed his steps toward me, although it was also easy to imagine that he had learned of my return from the agency handling my tickets. It is difficult to move without leaving traces, crumbs, behind. I invited him in because I had no choice, but what I really wanted, my real need, was to go out for a walk. There was a park just two blocks away. I thought that there, by the pines and poplars, I would be able to tell him. Beneath their branches. I would touch the bark of the trees and I would tell him, as always, the truth.

"So?" he said, tracing his index finger over the spines of some books.

"I warned you," I answered, turning my back to him.

He sat on the sofa, opening his legs.

"Everyone wants a forest sometimes," he muttered to

himself, looking at something through the window. "You have nice light in here," he said, changing—or perhaps circling back to—the subject.

I told him everything without pause. From beginning to end, using what I had written in the little notebook with the black cover. My report. My account of the facts. My voice, so calm. My hands, wringing inside my mind. The Taiga is, in fact, a disease, a syndrome. Some people flee the monotonous terrain even when they know they can't escape. Some people take flight, suicidal, without considering the speed, their goal, what lies beyond. Some of them dance. The more I talked the more incredible it all sounded to me. The more implausible. The angrier. He snatched the little notebook from me and, as he flipped through it, began to shout.

"Even falling out of love finally ends." Had I really told him that? My voice softer. Placating someone is also a spiritual exercise. Look at this: your knees. They are used for kneeling upon reality, also for crawling, terrified. You use them to sit on a lotus flower and say goodbye to the immensity.

. . .

I remember the dance floor. Above all, I remember the spines of all the trees, swaying slightly. The howling. I remember the thin red thread that stretched between lips, my lips, toward the snow, and from there to one of the three corners of the sky. I remember the clouds, so gray. Is there really a wild animal about to jump? Such delicate creatures. I remember the glass of the window, broken into so many pieces. My cheekbone. My forehead. I remember my mouth, toothless.

When she wondered what a bird would see through our windows, I would have wanted to tell her:

"Just like cats, of any kind, their idea of space is more elastic, less dependent on gravity than that of humans. It makes sense that time is also different for them, that this large window that separates us vibrates with questions whose answers or implications we ignore. Like we ignore who is asking or answering them."

XXII: A Closed Forest

I didn't hear him arrive, it's true. It wasn't until hours, maybe even days after, that I noticed his presence. "To prowl" is a stealthy verb. It hadn't been long since I'd left the hospital and I was just getting used to the new slowness of my movements. The different aches of my body. The subtle colors of my bruises. The bandages. Like everyone else, I had read the news in the papers. A wolf had escaped from a zoo located in the middle of a forest, a forest on the edge of a city. The security personnel had noticed the animal's disappearance during their routine inspection and, fearing the worst, had ordered that the forest be closed. But how do you do that? I wondered while reading the report. Do you close a forest the same way you close an envelope? Although they said it had been spotted among the trees, no source confirmed that it had been trapped. They said they expected things to return to normal but never specified what that meant. What things.

. . .

Was it even worse than they feared?

From a distance he looked like a dog with thick fur. Gray, in fact. Gray fur with darker tips, not quite black. His head slumping over his front paws added an air of weariness, or of belonging to someone. If someone had passed my door they would have thought, no doubt, that he was a domestic guard dog. A visible touch of loyalty or patience. The romance between master and pet in the glow of the afternoon sun. Time, its passage. Time that heals almost everything. In fact, I was going to ask him, "But what are you doing here?"—when I stopped dead in my tracks.

I remembered, then, the sound of his voice. The texture of his tongue. The way he talked about things, going around in circles. How the echo of his words lingered outside my ears before piercing my eardrum. The supple cartilage. The bone tissue. The soft skin. I saw his eyes. I let him see me. I didn't know what it meant when he sat up on all four paws. Was it compassion or grace that flowed from his golden eyes? We all carry a forest inside us, yes, kilometers and kilometers of birch, fir, cedars. A gray sky. Things that never change. I thought he would jump at any moment. I saw his jaw, his saliva. Teeth.

And then, air. Just air.

Yes, that's how it all went. That, as always, I told the truth. Yes. That I had.

December 31, 2011
At the foot of a volcano

XXIII: Playlist

Aphex Twin, *Rhubarb [on classical guitar]*
Einojuhani Rautavaara, *Cantus Arcticus*
Emancipator, *First Snow [Soon It Will Be Cold Enough]*
Sainkho Namtchylak, *The Snow Fall Without You [Cyberia]*

Foals, *Spanish Sahara [Total Life Forever]*
Fever Ray, *When I Grow Up [Fever Ray]*
Sainkho Namtchylak, *Ritual Reality [Stepmother City]*

Fever Ray, *The Wolf*
Sainkho Namtchylak, *Siberian One [Cyberia]*

Juk Juk, *No Faith*

Oval, *Drift [O]*
Mira Calix, *Eileo [Eyes Set Against the Sun]*
Lisa Gerrard, *Come Tenderness [The Silver Tree]*
Sainkho Namchylack, *Lilla Evening [Cyberia]*

Hauschka, *One Wish [Room to Expand]*

CRISTINA RIVERA GARZA has been the recipient of numerous awards, including a 2020 MacArthur "Genius" Grant for Fiction. Originally written in Spanish, her many books have been translated into English, French, Italian, Portuguese, Korean, and more. Born in Mexico in 1964, Rivera Garza has lived in the United States since 1989. She is Distinguished Professor in Hispanic Studies and Director of Creative Writing at the University of Houston.

SUZANNE JILL LEVINE has received many honors for her translations of Latin American literature. She is the author of *Manuel Puig and the Spider Woman: His Life and Fictions* (FSG) and *The Subversive Scribe: Translating Latin American Fiction* (Dalkey Archive Press). Her editions include the Penguin Paperback Classics series of Jorge Luis Borges's essays and poetry.

AVIVA KANA is a PhD candidate in Hispanic literature at the University of California, Santa Barbara. Her work focuses on Latin American literature, gender, translation, and applied linguistics. Her translations have been published in *Review: Literature and Arts of the Americas*, *PEN America*, *Latin American Literature Today*, and *Fiction*.

1. Renee Gladman *Event Factory*
2. Barbara Comyns *Who Was Changed and Who Was Dead*
3. Renee Gladman *The Ravickians*
4. Manuela Draeger *In the Time of the Blue Ball* (tr. Brian Evenson)
5. Azareen Van der Vliet Oloomi *Fra Keeler*
6. Suzanne Scanlon *Promising Young Women*
7. Renee Gladman *Ana Patova Crosses a Bridge*
8. Amina Cain *Creature*
9. Joanna Ruocco *Dan*
10. Nell Zink *The Wallcreeper*
11. Marianne Fritz *The Weight of Things* (tr. Adrian Nathan West)
12. Joanna Walsh *Vertigo*
13. Nathalie Léger *Suite for Barbara Loden* (tr. Natasha Lehrer & Cécile Menon)
14. Jen George *The Babysitter at Rest*
15. Leonora Carrington *The Complete Stories*
16. Renee Gladman *Houses of Ravicka*
17. Cristina Rivera Garza *The Taiga Syndrome* (tr. Aviva Kana & Suzanne Jill Levine)
18. Sabrina Orah Mark *Wild Milk*
19. Rosmarie Waldrop *The Hanky of Pippin's Daughter*
20. Marguerite Duras *Me & Other Writing* (tr. Olivia Baes & Emma Ramadan)
21. Nathalie Léger *Exposition* (tr. Amanda DeMarco)
22. Nathalie Léger *The White Dress* (tr. Natasha Lehrer)
23. Cristina Rivera Garza *New and Selected Stories* (tr. Sarah Booker, et al)
24. Caren Beilin *Revenge of the Scapegoat*
25. Amina Cain *A Horse at Night: On Writing*
26. Giada Scodellaro *Some of Them Will Carry Me*
27. Pip Adam *The New Animals*
28. Kate Briggs *The Long Form*